B49 082 973 2

KT-431-373

THERHAM LIBRARIES A

DISCARD

Spot's First Christmas

Eric Hill

It's Christmas Eve, Spot...

Wrap the presents neatly, Spot.

Be careful!

Who's outside?

Spot! Go to bed!

It's bedtime now, Spot.

Spot! Go to bed!

Spot is
asleep
at last!

Very early next morning . . .

A ball, a bone.

a brush. What else?

What a lovely blue collar, Spot.

Father Christmas brought it!

PUFFIN BOOKS

Published by the Penguin Group: London, New York,
Australia, Canada, India, New Zealand and South Africa
Penguin Books Ltd, Registered Offices:
80 Strand, London WC2R 0RL, England

puffinbooks.com

First published by William Heinemann Ltd, 1983
Published in Puffin Books 1986
25 27 29 30 28 26

Copyright © Eric Hill, 1983
All rights reserved

Printed and bound in Malaysia

ISBN–13: 978–0–14050–551–1